Our Needs and Wants

Mary Griffin

REAL LIFE readers™

Rosen Classroom™

New York

This is my home.

I need a home to live in.

This is a tent.

I want a tent to sleep in.

This is my food.

I need food to eat.

This is candy.

I want candy to eat.

It is cold.

Which coat do I need?

Needs	Wants

What do you need?

What do you want?

Words to Know

coat

tent